THE ROYAL MUSE

Copyright © 2020 by Judy McDonough

All rights reserved. Except for use in any review, the reproduction or utilization of this work in whole or in part in any form by any electronic, mechanical or other means, now known or hereinafter invented, including xerography, photocopying and recording, or in any information storage or retrieval system, is forbidden without the written permission of the publisher.

This is a work of fiction. Names, characters, places and incidents are either the product of the author's imagination or are used fictitiously, and any resemblance to actual persons, living or dead, business establishments, events or locales is entirely coincidental.

Printed in the USA.

Cover Design and Interior Format

2023

The ROYAL MUSE

For Alissa ⚜

JUDY MCDONOUGH

♡ Judy McDonough

For my boys.
Now you finally have something with
the correct spelling of your names.

Chapter 1

"Hey, Mom. No one's murdered me yet, and I haven't found any lost treasure." Melody answered her phone while hastily opening the living room windows of her newly inherited French Quarter residence. Early March in New Orleans was perfect open-window weather, especially now that Mardi Gras was past. "Though, I'm pretty sure I found a bottle of wine from the days of prohibition." She padded up the winding staircase to open the floor-to-ceiling shutter windows and glanced across the street at the vacant balcony still decorated for Carnival. She checked her watch.

Her mother chuckled. "Hey, honey. Glad you like your new digs. Maw Maw would be proud." Mom said. "Getting settled?"

"Yes. Finally," she mumbled.

"It's only been a few months. It takes time to make something your own. You're enjoying it, right?"

"Oh, absolutely! This place is amazing. I am the envy—and mystery—among all the starving artists in the city. They're all wondering how in the world I could afford such an extravagant and expensive condo." Melody filled a glass with ice water and checked across the street again, surprised at the disappointment she felt. Her mystifying neighbor must be running late. He'd usually made an appearance by now.

"Ah, yes. I'm a little covetous, myself. The perks of being the only grandchild. Your grandparents were what we called 'Old Money.'" She sighed. "I should've been nicer to your grandmother, God rest her soul."

Melody pressed her lips together and set her glass on the coffee table. She propped a fresh new canvas on her easel and smoothed her hand across the textured fabric as if greeting an old friend. "Don't be silly, she loved you. And I miss her, too. At least she passed peacefully in her sleep before the New Year. Though it is a shame she didn't get to enjoy one last Mardi Gras. She loved Carnival season."

"That she did." Her mom's voice trailed off wistfully.

"Besides, you have no reason to be jealous. She left you her fortune in diamonds and gemstones. No fake costume jewelry for Madam Estelle Landry."

"True, but it doesn't beat a million-dollar condo on Royal Street."

Melody practically hugged herself. "Yeah, you're right. I win." Her eyes fluttered toward movement on the railing of his balcony. Just a bird. She stuck her tongue out at the fat robin and went back to her business.

She vigorously shook her paint bottle before popping open the cap and breathing in the familiar scent. Thankfully, the condo had been furnished when she received it, which helped greatly considering Melody was coming fresh out of her parents' pool house and had no furniture.

Her grandmother had rented her condo out as an Air BnB over the past year while she stayed with her only son's family—Melody's dad—in their equally extravagant Garden District home. However, when she was nearing the end of her life, no more reservations were allowed. The condo hadn't been occupied since before Christmas, when it had been cleaned from the last tenant, and Melody moved into it in January.

Luckily, all she needed after scoring the keys

to the condo was to freshen it up a bit with her artistic touches, move her art supplies and clothes, and set up her studio in the guest bedroom upstairs. Some fresh paint and different art hanging on the walls, and the place was finally hers.

"Maybe since you already owned a lovely home she felt she could leave this one to her broke and homeless granddaughter. You're welcome here anytime." Melody grinned like the Grinch and added, "Especially when you feel like cooking."

"Of course. Have you spoken to Terry lately?"

How predictable of her mother to bring him up. Melody flopped back in her chair and closed her eyes, tapping the clean paintbrush against her forehead. "No, and I don't intend to think about that loser ever again. That's why they're called exes. He screwed up for the last time."

"Are you sure? He was such a nice boy."

"Mom, seriously?" She lurched forward and tossed the brushes onto the easel tray. "When we would go out together his right hand would be feeling other girls up while his left hand was in mine. Not to mention what all—or *who* all—he did when I *wasn't* with him. He was a scumbag. You were just fooled by his

THE ROYAL MUSE

charm. He had your number and knew how to use it."

"Maybe so. How 'bout I come cook for you Saturday evening? Blackened chicken fettuccine Alfredo. Your favorite."

Melody's mouth watered. "Yum. Can't wait. I think I might actually have all the ingredients for that in my kitchen."

"I'll bring the wine." She laughed. "And hand sanitizer," she added. "There's a nasty virus killing people in droves in China and Italy right now, and the news is saying it's only a matter of time before it's over here, so they're pushing hand-washing and sanitizer like crazy. I bought some extras I'll bring to you. Plus, I'm eager to cook in your kitchen. It's nicer than mine. Remember, you're not allowed to ever sell it. Your grandparents were adamant about keeping it in the family."

"Are you kidding? I would be crazy to give this place up. I'm a painter living in Art Central. The spoiled envy of every soul passing by taking pictures of my new digs and whatever creations I display on my lovely balcony."

Melody peeked through the sheer curtains at the still-empty balcony across the street. Her elusive musical neighbor hadn't yet set up for his weekly solo performance. The sounds she so eagerly needed to spark her creative flow.

Surely, he would come soon. He never missed a Thursday evening performance. Perhaps she was a little overzealous about his playing, but she didn't care. She had yet to see his face from the dimly lit distance, but it didn't matter. She'd already grown attached to him. She craved it. She was a junkie, and he was her dealer.

"The neighborhood is great. I love hearing the sounds of the city through my windows, especially at night." Dusk, in particular, she thought. When the soft melody of his trumpet stoked her artistic embers, igniting them like a raging wildfire. She'd already created four masterpieces. Two more would complete her collection.

"Well, be careful. Your dad and I are proud of you and happy Maw Maw left you the condo, but while it's a beautiful escape on the inside, it's still in the heart of the French Quarter. You've never lived away from us, and while Terry might have been a dirty cheater, I felt better knowing you had a man to protect you if need be. Now you're living alone right in the thick of strangers, thieves, and vagabonds looking for anything they can get for nothing."

Melody rolled her eyes. "Gosh, Mom. You sound like a snobby socialite. I always keep my doors locked, don't worry. My fridge, freezer, and pantry are stocked, thanks to you and Dad. I have plenty of paint and canvases, and I practically live upstairs in my studio next to the balcony anyway, so relax. I'm an introvert, remember? I rarely emerge from my cave."

She gave her love to her mother and checked the clock again. Should be any time now. She finished preparing her paint and put the base coat on her canvas, awaiting the flow of ideas like life's blood pulsing through her veins. She didn't know what it was, but the somewhat sorrowful tone of his trumpet provoked an intimacy that inspired and filled her heart with emotion. Was it possible to fall in love with someone she'd never met? She must be crazy. But she'd take crazy if it meant she could continue creating the beautiful masterpieces his music influenced.

She stretched out on the chaise lounge positioned between the shutter windows and closed her eyes to meditate and clear her mind. Why did her mother have to bring up Terry? That bastard stole three good years of her youth.

She inhaled slowly, filling her lungs all the way to the bottom until it burned, and released the breath equally as slow. She licked her lips and massaged her temples, working her fingers up into her hair.

Melody focused on singular noises, concentrating on all the various sounds trickling through the open windows. Muted voices danced alongside footsteps and laughter of the passersby below, and the soft hum of car engines poked through the crowds on the street providing a background ambience. A barking dog in the distance offset the faint rhythm of the bucket-drumming street performers a block away on Bourbon Street. Then, just in time, a soothing salve on the itchy scab of reality.

A trumpet trilled through the scale, warming up for its healing ballad.

Melody released a breath she hadn't realized she was holding and sat up with a smile. What mood would he be in tonight? Each song he'd played over the weeks had inspired different themed paintings, each matching the tone of his song choice and perfectly reflecting her scorned mood at this stage in her life.

Throughout the week, in the days between performances, she found herself humming—and sometimes singing loudly—songs she wished he would masterfully play for her. Lately, she enjoyed harmonizing with him—as good as she could harmonize to original songs she didn't know—as his sounds filled the streets. Filled her space. Filled her soul.

She scurried to her chair and picked up her brush, twirling it between her fingers to allow the energy of the music to flow through it, sparking the magic within her that she devoured every Thursday evening through his melodic nocturne. It was time to channel her gift and let her art harmonize with his soul.

Chapter 2

REECE THOMAS SIPPED his coffee and cleaned the valves of his trumpet from the chair just inside his open window, occasionally peeking across the street toward the lavish condo Old Lady Landry used to own. He had finally come to the conclusion the songbird who currently occupied it was no temporary vacationer. He'd heard about Estelle Landry's passing just before Christmas, saddened that he hadn't had a chance to say goodbye to the woman who always offered a wave when she saw him. But then the blonde bombshell showed up. She'd been there for a few months now. A relative, perhaps?

He polished the bell of the instrument until he could see his reflection, and then carefully placed it in the velvet-lined case. He opted to spend his day off cleaning his apartment and preparing for the weekend while his roommate was out of town. The wedding gig his band had booked would hopefully get them more exposure, but he'd prefer funerals to weddings these days. The last wedding he'd attended almost killed him.

Just as his mood started to tank thinking about the past two years of misery, the most beautiful sound trickled through his open windows. She was singing again. He couldn't hear the music, but her voice reverberated the lyrics loudly through the old building. A familiar, upbeat nineties song. Alanis Morissette, in fact. He chuckled. She *oughta know* how much he enjoyed her singing.

He quietly hummed along with her chorus while unloading his dishwasher, and then the song changed to another nineties tune from her playlist. This time it was a Celine Dion ballad really showcasing her vocals. This choice of music vastly differed from her normal tastes, and seemed peculiar considering the songs probably came out around the time she was born. Vintage. Maybe it was cleaning day for her, too. He paused, taking much longer to dry a glass than necessary, while he allowed her smooth, pitch-perfect instrument to caress his ears. Did she realize her gift?

How could he learn more about her without coming across as a stalker? He was afraid to let her know he could hear her for fear she'd be embarrassed and stop singing. As far as he could tell she enjoyed his trumpet playing, so he didn't feel bad about practicing on his balcony every Thursday. In fact, he'd caught her singing along with him a few times when he covered well-known songs.

He finished his dishes and wiped his counters. The place was clean, no thanks to his lazy roommate brother, and all he had left to do was…nothing. Sit. Write. Draw. Read. None of those struck his fancy. He busted out some push-ups and sit-ups, finishing with a five-minute plank. For the past two years he'd worked out daily in his apartment, nothing ridiculous, just some calisthenics and dumbbells to keep fit. He tried to go for a three-mile run at least three times a week. Something to keep him sane. Focusing on his health and strength had become a priority after the incident. His hand subconsciously traced the five-inch scar stretching across his abdomen. A painful reminder to never be weak again.

Movement from across the way caught his attention, so he settled back into a corner to observe, his deltoids twitching from their recent stimulation. His little songbird was setting up an easel in the sunshine, positioning it so the rays were a spotlight on an oversized canvas that faced him. It seemed a bit difficult to maneuver with her petite stature. The canvas was almost as big as she was. Acrylic dried quickly, so if she was setting it out to dry it must be oil paint. Reece squinted to see if he could identify details of the painting. Two people walking hand-in-hand on a French Quarter street.

Her normally long, straight hair was swept up into a sloppy blonde pile on top of her head, allowing him to see her face for the first time in the daylight. Early-to-mid-twenties, it was hard to tell. But the large blue eyes and rounded cheekbones that filled the small space looked almost animé, making her seem younger. Innocent. Those big baby blues were centered over a dainty little nose and full pink lips that matched her powder pink shirt. Cuteness overload.

She turned to face him, causing him to slink further into the shadows of his curtains like a Peeping Tom. Had she spotted him? His heart raced and his stomach sank. Had she felt him watching her? Why was he so nervous? He'd been around beautiful women before. He'd actually been married to one, however brief it may have been. Then she ripped his heart out and ate it like the wedding cake.

But this woman…this one affected him differently. She touched his soul with song, which was something no other woman had ever done. How was it possible to feel so strongly for someone to whom he'd never spoken a word?

She shaded her eyes with one hand and pretended she was looking along the sidewalks, but her eyes kept flittering back to his balcony as if she didn't want to be obvious. An old sensation he hadn't felt in ages fluttered through his chest. Was she as interested in him as he was her? Reece was committed now. No going back. He had to know her.

"Who are you, little songbird?" he murmured. She pulled at her shirttail and cursed at the palm-sized smudge of black paint.

She stormed back inside, stripping her shirt off as she walked and exposing her bare back before ducking into the condo. Heat flushed his face and then headed southbound, filling the void of another neglected area. She was out of sight, but her toned, braless back was now committed to memory. His deprived, testosterone-filled imagination ran wild. He'd wanted to know more about her before, when he'd only heard her amazing voice and song choices, but now… Her absence left a wanton desire to shout for her to come back. To come over. A name. For now, he would settle for her name.

As if she read his mind, she came back outside in a tattered old T-shirt and walked to the other end of her balcony carrying a second easel. She set up another oversized canvas, more carefully this time, depicting another French Quarter street. This one had a different vibe with a street performer shouting angrily at someone passing by as if they'd stolen from his…wait a sec. Reece leaned forward to see it better, risking the reveal of his position. He squinted. There was something familiar about that one he hadn't recognized in the other. It was *his* street. Royal Street. Her impressive talent had no limits. In what other areas was she skilled?

While he'd been focused on her second painting, she had draped a large vinyl banner over the railing in between her paintings, securing the metal eye hooks to the wrought iron bars with zip ties. An art show at the gallery down the street. She was an artist by trade, not hobby. Of course. A creative soul. That made perfect sense, and it explained the instant connection he felt to her and her love for music.

Reece took advantage of her distraction while hanging the sign and sprinted to his laptop. He scoured the web for information about this art gallery and its scheduled art shows. If he were to bump into her at the show it would offer an organic opportunity to learn more about her and potentially build from there.

March twenty-first, the date her sign advertised, would feature The Royal Muse Collection up for auction. Oil paintings by Melody Landry. Ten more days.

Melody… What a fitting title for the lovely little songbird who had flitted into his life and given it purpose once again.

Chapter 3

MELODY LOOKED OVER the five paintings she had already created thanks to her enigmatic neighbor's masterful trumpeting. Louis Armstrong would be envious of this guy's talent, though she doubted ol' Louis would enjoy the anguish seeping through the notes. What had broken him so strongly that he only felt moved to play melancholy music? She desperately wanted to find out so she could…comfort him.

She must be nuts. Why did she feel compelled to comfort someone she'd never physically met in person? But then again, she felt as if she knew him intimately, knew his deepest, darkest secrets, and that she was indebted to protecting him from such heartache. Yeah, she was certifiably insane. With her luck, he was a psychopath who would strangle her and feed her body to the gators. But he played a mean trumpet.

No, she refused to believe he was dangerous. Anyone who cared so deeply for something as insignificant as a trumpet and handled it as if it were a precious and fragile keepsake, caressing it like erotic foreplay with a lover, and playing the fiery hell out of it couldn't possibly be bad.

Her mother had cooked for her last week, and stopped by two days ago to drop off enough casseroles to feed an army. She called them freezer meals, but her freezer was already full from the monster-load of groceries her father had ordered for her. It was a miracle she'd been able to squeeze them into her fridge.

Melody exhaled and dragged her palm down her face before stacking her masterpiece from last week on the top of the pile, face up, in case there were any small bits that weren't dry. She propped up a blank canvas for her sixth and final piece to the compilation. It was Thursday, after all, and with any luck her mysterious neighbor would assist in the completion to her Royal Muse Collection. The collective theme was no doubt bitter and scorned, and possibly even somber, but that's how she'd been feeling lately after her nasty breakup with what's-his-name. Besides, it accompanied the dismal post-carnival mood of the city.

Her worrywart mother had called her yesterday to warn her about a strain of coronavirus called COVID-19 that had infiltrated the city, and she adamantly reminded her to wash her hands, don't touch her face, clean every commonly used surface like doorknobs, cell phone, credit cards, and so on. Basically, as if the apocalypse was coming. Melody's father was a doctor, so he'd seen several cases come through. It explained the giant grocery and household items delivered to her yesterday from her dad. She'd been confused about the enormous pack of toilet paper and paper towels considering she lived alone.

Melody opened her pantry that was now bursting at the seams and straightened the cans of tuna so they all faced the same direction. With all this food she would be set until fall. Warmth spread over her. Her pops was still taking care of her. She smiled and grabbed the croutons for her salad. While she ate, she allowed her mind to drift into deep daydreaming.

There were still a few hours left before showtime, and she had no idea what she would paint tonight. The other nights she'd had some inkling of a scene; she only needed his song choice to nail down the mood. Like clockwork, he impeccably delivered the feeling she wished to portray in the art, as if he'd plucked it from the sea of emotions in her head. A sea from which she couldn't possibly choose just one on her own.

She washed and rinsed her bowl and put it in the dish drainer. The reality of her situation had crept in like an unwanted guest, and between the dreary news reports and her parents' dire, Apocalyptic warnings, all the bottled-up emotions were ready to spew out of her. The hurricane of mood swings was strong this week, and she considered putting away her paints and watching a sad movie that matched her mood. She only hoped her muse would deliver the perfect song as he had so many times before.

She stretched out on the love seat and closed her eyes. When she opened them again, it was dark. Once she realized what she'd done she scurried, somewhat disoriented, to the window for a peek. Had she missed him through her zombie nap?

Her fellow had already set up his chair with the gleaning trumpet propped bell down, reflecting the gas lamps that flanked his balcony doors. A highball glass with a double pour of amber liquid sat on a TV tray next to his chair. Melody's mouth curved downward in commiserating agreement. Rough day. She totally felt that vibe.

He emerged with a bottle of the same amber liquid, startling her with his sudden appearance, and she lurched backward and off-balance. She slid off the chaise lounge in what had to be slow motion, knocked over a tray full of paint bottles and brushes, as well as a full cup of brush water, and landed with a *thunk* against the hard, wooden floor.

She groaned and froze in place. She didn't even want to know if he heard—or God forbid saw—her flub. *Smooth, Mel. Really*. She crawled into the kitchen for a towel to soak up the water and couldn't resist a peek to check if he'd seen her. Her eyes met his for the first time in the five weeks since he'd started his serenades, and she couldn't look away from their instant connection.

He had definitely witnessed her graceless display.

Wait a minute—was he smiling at her?

A grin involuntarily spread across her flaming face, and she was thankful for the darkness. Hoping her crimson cheeks were disguised by the flickering reflections of her own gas balcony lanterns, she offered a shy wave. He dipped his chin to nod a hello, but his amusement and twinkling eyes didn't dull the overwhelming sadness bleeding from his handsome features.

Melody slinked back inside in hopes her humiliating moment wouldn't deter his decision to perform and settled onto her painting stool. Her heart still pounded, but she couldn't get his attractive face out of her mind. Before seeing him, she'd have bet money he was around forty-five based on his body language and song choices, but the man she saw tonight couldn't be more than thirty. He was striking with his dark features and mysterious expression. She couldn't tell much about his hair for the newsboy hat he wore, only that it touched his shoulders.

His expansive, muscular shoulders.

The slow, solemn sounds reverberating through the still night air were later than usual, and not the normal trilling warm-up with which he usually started. This sound was one of grief and torment. The haunting sound of despair in a familiar song she normally enjoyed. She'd never heard Nat King Cole's "Nature Boy" quite like this, and she loved it even more now. It filled the night air like smoke from a wildfire.

She scrambled for the proper paintbrush while ideas flashed through her brain like a strobe light. She knew exactly what she would paint as his music performed its usual duty, percolating magic through her body in the form of art.

He only played the one song tonight, but he sat quietly on his balcony and sipped his drink as he stared in her direction. She made sure her canvas was blocked from his view and that she faced him back in case he needed her for inspiration as much as she needed him. Whatever happened, she didn't want him to see what she painted. Not until it was finished, at least. And she wouldn't stop until she was finished with the first layer. She would need to allow enough time for drying in between layers, and she only had five days before the art show, so it needed to be completely dry by then. Maybe by that time she would be ready to meet her secret crush in person. Ready to reveal—even if through a simple thank-you note—how much she appreciated his gift. Ready to reveal her work to him. To reveal her soul.

Maybe.

Chapter 4

⚜

REECE SQUINTED FROM the intrusive sun lurching him from his slumber as his brother, Rowen, yanked the curtains back from both shutter windows in his bedroom.

"Wakey, wakey, sleeping beauty. Time to rise and shine."

He'd never hated his roommate before, but this constituted retaliation. He threw a pillow at him, but it didn't have the force behind it he thought he'd extended. "What the… Seriously, dude? Get the hell outta here." Reece reached for his phone on the bedside table. Ten 'til nine. Guess it was probably time to get up, but his dry mouth and pounding head suggested otherwise.

"March sixteenth. You had all day yesterday to mourn, and I promised you last year I would personally see to it you didn't drown in a bottle for weeks—or months," Rowen grumbled. "Never again. So"—he clapped his hands emphasizing the throbbing sensation in Reece's head— "get your lazy butt up and let's go for a grocery run."

Reece flipped him the bird on his nosedive into his fluffy pillow. "Go away." His muffled voice had about as much authority to it as his pillow toss had a few minutes before.

"Look," Rowen sighed. "I miss them, too. But it's been two years. You can't keep doing this to yourself. Regan wouldn't have wanted that, and neither would Mom."

Reece knew he was right, but it didn't make it easier. "I drank too much last night."

"All the more reason to get up and get your blood pumping. Flush your system. Let's go." Rowen stripped the covers off of Reece and grabbed his ankle, pulling all one hundred and eighty pounds of him off the bed and onto the floor. Reece managed to get a good kick in before Rowen trotted out of the room, laughing. Bastard. He propped his elbows onto his knees and cradled his head. It felt like it was made of glass that could shatter at the slightest touch or sound.

"Here." Rowen held out a bottle of water and three ibuprofen tablets. "The city is about to shut down because of this damn virus, so let's get out and buy some groceries before it does."

Reece frowned, the gesture causing more discomfort to his achy eyes. "What virus?"

"COVID-19. Remember, we heard about it a couple of weeks ago and blew it off because it was happening on the other side of the world. Well, it spread like wildfire, and now it's over here in the good ol' U.S. of A. It just finished wreaking havoc in China and Italy to the point they're having to make decisions about who lives or dies because they're out of space and ventilators. And thanks to Mardi Gras, a cess pool of drunk tourists, and stubborn locals refusing to abide by the social distancing orders, New Orleans is one of the hardest hit."

"What is it, like, the plague?"

"Pneumonia or some kind of respiratory thing, but it's sure spreading like the plague. They're using the word *pandemic*. We need groceries." He held up a finger. "And toilet paper. Apparently, that crap is flying off the shelves." Rowen laughed at his pun. "People are hoarding it like they all just ate cheap Mexican food." He stripped Reece's bed and plopped the dirty sheets in his lap. "Seriously, though, this virus is legit. We need to clean and sanitize everything."

"Who are you and what have you done with my roommate? You know, the slob who likes to sleep late and never watches the news."

"I'm a changed man now. Harley gave me a new outlook on life. She gave me a reason to care."

"She gave you a ride on dat booty," Reece mumbled.

Rowen peeked his head around the corner and grinned. "That, too."

"Called it," Reece said, and slowly rose from the floor with his sheets. "I knew you'd be whipped before long. What's it been, a month?" He added his sheets to the other ones under the scalding water filling the washing machine. "I'm gonna shower. Give me twenty minutes."

"You have ten. Bust a move," Rowen demanded.

"Dude, I'm older. I'll take as long as I want and you can kiss my ass."

"Ten minutes." Rowen sang the words as he sprayed the kitchen counters with Clorox and scrubbed.

He would make it a twenty-minute shower if it killed him. Little turd needed to remember his place. Reece dragged his feet into the bathroom and flinched when he looked in the mirror. Good thing he hadn't looked like that when his songbird caught him on the balcony. Though he'd already had two glasses of bourbon, so it was entirely possible he had.

He'd clearly caught her by surprise. It had taken all his control not to laugh out loud when Melody fell, but a part of him wanted to rush to her aid and kiss her boo-boos. He stamped that part out pretty quickly, though. Last night wasn't the night for romance. It was a night for mourning. And lots of alcohol to numb the pain and constant reminders.

The hot water beat down on his tense muscles. He tended to carry his stress like Atlas with the weight of the world on his shoulders. Reece replayed the scene from last night as best as he could remember. She looked great. Her hair was a hot mess, like she'd just woken up, but it somehow looked styled. Her oversized sweatshirt had slid to one side, exposing a perfectly toned and feminine shoulder. Her pale skin looked bronze from the soft glow of the gas lantern, and it looked soft as butter. He imagined it felt that soft, too.

And she'd smiled at him. Not just any smile. It was flirty. She was into him, but how? She knew nothing about him. Maybe he could fix that by knocking on her door and introducing himself. After all, it wasn't strange for neighbors to do that, right?

Maybe he'd bake her some brownies. With his luck she was vegan or on some crazy diet that didn't allow carbs or sugar…or flavor. He'd figure all that out later when he had a clearer head. And groceries.

Her art show this week would be a good topic to spark conversation. He could get her talking about herself. People generally liked talking about themselves. Not him. He'd rather discuss quantum physics than reveal anything personal. He didn't even want to know details about his own psyche, so why on earth would anyone else? No need to subject perfectly nice people to the dark and dreary abyss of his soul.

Three loud bangs on the door yanked him from his reverie. "Come on, man. You're burning daylight."

"The more you bug me the longer it's going to be. Go bang something else."

He finished soaping up and rinsed off with renewed anticipation. His hands almost trembled with excitement as he shut off the faucet. He dried at record speed and emerged from the steamy bathroom to find Rowen standing with crossed arms and a smug expression. He nodded toward Reece's semi-aroused state after thinking about Melody.

"Have a good time in there?"

"Piss off." He stormed past his brother and

pulled some clothes from his dresser.

"What's her name?"

"Who?"

"The girl you were beating off to. She has a name, right? And a pulse?"

Reece glared at him. "There is no girl, and I wasn't beating off, perv. Don't you have anything better to do than annoy me?"

Rowen held up his hands in surrender. "Not today, bro. I told you. Today is dedicated to you and your well-being. And groceries, because I'm hungry, and I need more than a Slim Jim and Pop Tarts." He smirked. "Is she hot?"

Reece stormed past him and slipped his sneakers on. "I'm not having this conversation with you right now." He grabbed his reusable grocery bags and keys and walked out without looking back.

Rowen was right behind him. "So there *is* a girl. I knew it. It's the only thing that could have you this moody and excited at the same time. Not to mention it's the first time since the accident that I've seen a spark in your eyes."

"*Incident*," Reece corrected him. "It was no accident, believe me."

"Fair enough." They walked in silence to the grocery a couple of blocks down, and Reece had to keep checking to see if his brother

THE ROYAL MUSE 37

was conscious. He never went this long without talking or at least spewing judgy sarcasm about random people. When they walked into the grocery, they both stopped in their tracks. It looked like the day before a hurricane was supposed to hit. People were everywhere pushing and cutting each other off, and several of the paper goods shelves were dwindling, with only a few items left. Canned meat and vegetables were being snatched almost in sync.

"You go left, I'll go right, grab the first things your hands touch." Rowen pushed a basket toward him and grabbed one for himself.

"Don't knock any old people over, and don't touch your face," Reece added. He had been through his fair share of emergencies and panic buyers when he'd worked at a Rouse's Grocery Store for a few years in his early twenties, but in all his twenty-nine years he'd never seen things this bad for no apparent reason. What the hell kind of virus was this?

Chapter 5

MELODY STARED AT the television, trying to make sense of everything the news anchors just said. A pandemic? Her parents had been right. Everything was closing, people were losing their jobs, any occupation that involved human contact but wasn't essential was instructed to close. Salons, tattoo parlors, massage therapy clinics…and art galleries. Every art gallery in the city had closed only four days before her show was to be held. This was a nightmare. Her phone buzzed next to her.

"Hello?"

"Mel, it's Daniel. Did you hear the latest? We have to close the gallery."

"I heard. That sucks so bad. What am I going to do?"

"I have an idea. What about a virtual art

show? We can advertise it on our website, all over social media, and put a sign in the window in case people come by. I'll have a professional photographer take pictures of your paintings, and we can do an online auction for each one every hour from two o'clock until eight o'clock. Also, I'm going to donate the gallery's percentage of the proceeds to hospitals and first responders to buy the supplies they need to protect them against COVID-19. Do you want to do the same? It might get us more traffic if it's charitable. What do you think?"

Melody shrugged before she remembered Daniel couldn't see her, so she swallowed the lump in her throat. "Sure, of course. Whatever you think will work best to draw more bids. Do you really think people will log into a website to shop for art? I mean, that's something that is usually best viewed in person to see the dimension and feel of it, and people are losing their jobs right now. Art is not exactly a necessity for living."

"Trust me, people are freaking out about this whole thing everywhere. An escape is exactly what they want. Even museums across the world—the Louvre, the Smithsonian—are all offering free online virtual tours. People want to help. While we can't give your art away for free, donating it to the greater good of the medical professionals working tirelessly to help sick and dying patients is one way people can help without risking their lives. It'll work."

Melody dabbed her finger on the paint of her latest creation to see if it had dried. "I finished my last piece last night, so they'll be ready in a few more days after they've all dried. I hope you're right and people take the time to log in to an art gallery."

"They have nothing but time, honey. Schools and businesses are closed, people are working from home. Everyone is doing things online. I mean, there are the normal crazies who think it's no big deal and still come out around people, but have you looked outside lately? The government has issued an order for people to stay home. This place is a ghost town compared to what it usually is. And it's charitable, so they'll feel good about spending their money." Daniel laughed while Melody went out on her balcony, and her jaw literally dropped open. The streets were empty, with only the random straggler walking the sidewalk, and businesses were locked up and boarded shut.

"What the…"

"Right. I was thinking we could do a live video of you explaining each painting, your

The Royal Muse

inspiration, et cetera. Maybe what went into creating the mood of the painting. The same kind of things you would be telling people at the art show. We can even allow people to comment or live-chat if they have questions, and then at the end of the hour we will do a ten-minute auction to sell them."

"Sounds like you have it all figured out."

"You know me, I'm all about plan B. I had this in mind when I first heard about this thing. If I come up with something even better, we'll do that instead. I should've already had the pictures taken just in case, but I farted around and ran out of time."

"Yeah, well, nobody's perfect." Melody's attempt at humor fell flat.

"Tell me about it. So, I'll send a photographer over to your place tonight to take pics. Do you have a well-lit area to display them for the pictures, or do you need to bring the paintings into the studio?"

"No, I have a wall with track lighting. It should be fine. I'd rather not transport them just yet because my latest one isn't completely dry."

"Got it. He'll be there at six tonight."

Melody hung up and leaned on her railing. This was crazy. She took the opportunity to really look at her neighbor's balcony, as well as his first-floor entry. Did he have a roommate or live alone? What was his name? What was his job? Did he play in a band, or was trumpet a hobby? She had so many questions but no time to ask them now. She had to get her paintings set up and write out the descriptions of each one in such a way people would be drawn to them without actually being able to see them in person.

As she turned to go inside, a crash caught her attention. Glass breaking followed by shouting. She spun to see where it had come from and realized it was on the bottom floor of her handsome trumpet player's place.

"I told you last week to get some groceries because I was stuck in the office with a mountain of paperwork, but no, you were too damned busy drinking your feelings at your little pity party to worry about responsibilities."

"Screw you, dude. Get off my ass. I pay my half of the rent, and I do all the cooking and cleaning—"

"Seriously? Have you looked at your room? That place is a breeding ground for bacteria. It's amazing we don't already have the virus. Guess it's a good damn thing you never go anywhere around other human beings."

The string of curse words that followed

would have made a whole ship of sailors blush. Melody had never heard the F-word used in so many creative ways before. It was kind of impressive.

"This week has always sucked for me and you know it. Besides, I am the germaphobe who normally cleans around here. So I've had a few bad days. Who gives a shit? Just because Harley has you by the balls and in touch with your feminine side these days doesn't mean you can criticize my behavior."

"I'm starving! What are we going to eat for dinner tonight? Pork and beans? God knows you bought plenty of that trash the last time you actually went shopping. We don't even have any Ramen Noodles because the damned grocery was empty. This is bullshit!"

Another crash. She'd heard of people being hangry—so hungry they're angry—before, but she never actually witnessed it.

"Break something else and I'll kick your ass! You're pissing me off."

"Good! At least you're feeling something for once! It's about time. I've been living with a zombie for two years."

"Whatever. Go have your temper tantrum on your side of the apartment and stop breaking all my shit."

"Me? You want to criticize my mood? Look

in the mirror! Regan would've kicked your ass with a frying pan by now and told you to stop being such a crybaby. I'll say it for the thousandth time. What happened wasn't your fault, so quit wallowing and get on with your life."

Melody slowly crept back inside her condo in shock. Either they were brothers or lovers, and likely not the latter from the mention of Harley having one of them by the balls. She couldn't tell whose voice was whose because they were hidden by the curtains. Her bet was brothers…or just roommates.

She grabbed a notebook and pen and begrudgingly sat in front of her first painting, trying to focus on her work rather than being a nosy neighbor. This was the first of six paintings in her Royal Muse Collection. A collaboration of images she'd personally noticed, all on Royal Street. This particular painting was of something she witnessed a little farther down Royal before she moved into the condo.

It was a scene of a crying homeless guy sitting outside a souvenir shop and getting yelled at by the owner to move while people stood by and watched. She'd been at a restaurant across the street having coffee and beignets when she heard the altercation. She sketched the scene on the back of a receipt in her purse so she would remember details. The poor, dejected expression of the homeless guy, and the angry humiliation of the store owner because of the customers who had crossed the street to avoid having to walk by the vagrant. She titled this one: A Royal Shame.

The second painting was titled quite literally: A Royal Pain in the Ass. A tragic and heartbreaking occasion that almost had her speaking out. It was of a mule-drawn carriage and the miserable, exhausted donkey after a long day of hauling people around. The poor thing foamed at the mouth, limped, and tugged on the straps connected all around it while its driver continued flapping her jaws about the haunted Lalaurie mansion to the tourists. Melody felt sorry for the animal that looked as exhausted as its driver. She hoped the mule got extra carrots and oats in the evening, but she doubted it.

The third painting was one of her favorites. It was titled: The Royal Blues and depicted a mournful occasion that is celebrated unlike anywhere else in the world. A New Orleans funeral. She'd been in the art gallery and heard the band's bluesy rendition of *A Closer Walk with Thee* as they neared the shop. She marveled at the people dancing their way down the street, holding umbrellas and handkerchiefs all while tears streamed down their faces as a carriage toted the casket for one last parade. They were saddened by the loss of their loved one but celebrated the full life that had been lived.

Her fourth scene was created after a rotten day. She was in a mood, mad at the world, and seeing this had set her off. She was on her way home with arms full of grocery bags, and she noticed a commotion between two or three people.

A silver-painted street performer lay frozen in a humorous-yet-compromising position, unable to move easily. He waited for people to donate money in his vintage top hat placed before him. Melody admired his ability to lie so still while a plethora of passing people posed with him, skittishly dropped money in his hat as if he would jump-scare them, pointed and laughed, spewed derogatory comments, and shook their judgmental heads.

What she hadn't expected was the jerk thief who slinked in, pretended to donate money, but instead grabbed the hat and ran like the coward he was. She watched as the street performer struggled to get up—stiff from being frozen in position for who knows how long—to chase after him, but the quick thief had escaped unscathed and unnoticed by anyone but her and the poor performer. The crushed, dejected, and betrayed look on his face haunted her dreams for days after that while she painted the recreation.

Melody finished marking down her comments about the painting and moved on to the next, blankly staring at it while it stirred a pit of unsettled anger in her gut. A clap of thunder outside commanded her attention. The skies had opened up, and the streets were rapidly collecting water. She set her notebook down with an irritated slap, tossing the pen atop her markings, and quickly closed the windows. Her head ached and this part of reliving the inspiration for the paintings only exacerbated the throbbing. She wished her music man would start playing right now to soften the blow of the next piece, but it wasn't his usual performance day, so she sucked it up and went back to work.

The fifth painting hit too close to home for her. It was aptly titled: The Royal Douche. The inspiration lying behind this one was a mixture of something she'd witnessed and something she'd experienced.

She'd been walking down Royal with her then-boyfriend explaining all the different styles of art hanging in the windows of the galleries. They'd passed a couple walking hand-in-hand and seemingly in love. Only, the guy's focus lingered a little too long on Melody's ample bosom before finally landing on her face. She'd initially thought he was reading her shirt until she realized there were no pictures or writing on her solid-colored blouse. Then his hand landed on Melody's left butt cheek and squeezed.

The violation stopped her in her tracks. She turned and shouted a string of colorful language and accusations at the jerk before looking at her boyfriend, Terry, in expectation. Rather than defending her honor and pummeling the douche-bag, he instead patronized Melody's "misinterpretation" of the "brush" of the guy's hand as they'd passed on the narrow sidewalk and suggested she stop overreacting for attention.

As Melody stood with mouth agape, unbelieving of the betrayal that just happened, the guy nodded his appreciation of Terry as they left. The smirk he wore was a knife to her heart. It wasn't until a couple of weeks later she found out that her asshole boyfriend had been doing the same kind of stuff to other women when they were dancing in clubs. One hand on her and the other groping some poor, unsuspecting female nearby. Thank goodness for the girls who pointed it out right in front of her or she'd never have known and would've missed the opportunity to slap him on the dance floor in front of God and everybody. Much to her pleasure the bouncer escorted him out, but her three-year relationship was ruined. Washed down the drain like blood left at a crime scene.

This painting reflected the scene from the street. The act of betrayal that should've been her first clue.

Melody forcibly unclenched her jaw and moved on to her final and absolute favorite painting in the collection: The Royal Lullaby. Just looking at it eased her anxiety and improved her mood. The theme of this one was self-explanatory. Well, to her, at least. It was a perfect depiction of her loyal, somber trumpeter who played his tragic anthems for her every Thursday evening. Her muse. The one thing that got her blood and creativity flowing but blew her mind in the same breath. Why was he so sad? What had caused his pain? How could she help to ease it?

She gently touched a glob of oil paint near the dripping music notes floating from the bell of his instrument. Not quite dry, but close. She'd purposely smeared the music notes so they looked wet and blurry as if they wept.

The blue hues combined with the golden reflections of the gas lanterns on the wet streets below emitted the sadness bleeding from his trumpet. But it was the love-filled expression from the girl in the shadows across the street that represented the way his music touched the hearts around him.

Melody brushed her fingertips across the goose bumps on her arms and cradled herself. His music embraced her. It wrapped its soft, fuzzy wings around her wounded soul and comforted her emptiness and heartache. The fear that no one would ever understand her depth and the very essence of what made her who she was. She truly believed he would get it. If she ever actually developed the courage to meet him in real life.

She had so many questions. Who was the Regan mentioned? What was she to Melody's trumpet player? She assumed the roommate was the one Harley had by the balls. At least she hoped. Were he and his roommate related or just close friends? What had happened to cause him to wallow in grief or self-pity? Why wasn't he able to let it go, whatever it was that wasn't his fault?

The doorbell rang, interrupting her concentration, and she realized it was six o'clock. Crap! It's raining! She flew down the stairs, hardly touching the steps, and flung the door open to let Daniel's photographer inside. The rain furiously pounded the sidewalk, coming down in sheets. Before Melody closed the door, a face with large, round, deep-set eyes watched her from inside the apartment across the street. As quickly as it appeared, it disappeared.

Chapter 6

❧

THE FLASHING INSIDE her condo looked like a lightning storm. What, exactly, was the dude taking pictures of at this time of night? Reece assumed it was a photographer, judging by the amount of equipment and flash boxes he'd struggled to get out of the rain all at once. He bit back his jealousy and opened the fridge for the fiftieth time. His annoying stomach hadn't stopped growling at him for over an hour. His refrigerator literally contained a six-pack of beer, a jar of pickle spears, mustard, ketchup, and a can of biscuits. He moved to the pantry and grabbed the two cans of pork and beans they had left and heated them in a saucepan. He put the biscuits on a cookie sheet and preheated the oven.

"What is that?" Rowen asked as he pulled an Endymion parade cup from the dishwasher and checked the inside to see if it was clean.

"Beans and biscuits. The last of our groceries."

"Nice. Wonder why that is?"

"Don't start."

"Whatever." He filled the cup with ice. "I think the restaurants are still serving take-out orders. I'm sure the grocery will have a new shipment soon. They have to. They've been picked dry like a turkey carcass at Thanksgiving." He held the cup under the faucet and filled it.

Reece nodded. "I called Rouse's this morning. They're supposed to get their weekly shipment Friday morning."

Rowen's hand stopped midway to his mouth. "It's Monday."

"I know."

He gulped his water down and refilled the cup. "Look, I'll see if Harley has any food. Maybe we can eat over at her place."

Reece shook his head. "Nope, not me. You go ahead. I'll be fine. We have some pretzels chips and peanut butter left in the pantry. That'll hold me over."

His brother cocked a disbelieving brow. "For what…an hour?" He laughed. "There's being prideful and then there's being stupid."

"How's business?"

"Good. Great, in fact." Rowen grinned. "No shortage of people wanting to sue other people. And, fortunately for me, being a bankruptcy lawyer at a time like this doesn't suck. Luckily I can do most everything remotely from home. No exposure to people means no sharing of germs. You never go anywhere or talk to anyone, so we should be okay from this virus."

"Do you think it's as bad as everyone's making out to be?"

Rowen shrugged. "Who knows? Probably not, but I've never seen the city this dead before."

"It's all that's on the news. Can't find a single channel not talking about it."

"They say it's most dangerous to young kids and old people. Have you talked to Dad?"

"Not since this whole crazy pandemic started. I know he's working from home." Reece popped open a beer. "But I swear if I hear COVID-19 or Coronavirus one more time I might vomit."

His brother eyed the bottle as Reece raised it to his mouth. "I'll bet he has food."

Reece swallowed the hoppy liquid and grimaced. He wasn't much of a beer drinker. He much preferred the hard stuff. "If you count week-old pizza leftovers and stale bread."

"I'm gonna call him." Rowen pulled his phone from his pocket.

"Suit yourself." He walked up the stairs to his bedroom and checked across the street again. His clock said quarter after seven. How long did a photography session usually last? He took another long pull from his bottle and nearly choked when her door popped open and her eyes zeroed in on his. He turned just in time, he hoped, that she hadn't seen him.

He clicked on his playlist, stripped off his shirt, and picked up the book near his bed. The melody of his favorite jazz band filled the room as he flipped to the dog-eared page. He had to do something to get his mind off of Melody before he became a full-blown stalker. She had consumed his thoughts over the past few weeks, and it was affecting his concentration.

What did it matter, though? His band hadn't gotten any gigs since the virus took hold of everything, so it wasn't like he had shit else to do. He had enough money saved from his lack of social life the past few years that he could afford to live without a job and still pay his bills and buy groceries—if the stores ever got any back in stock.

Rowen called for him to come downstairs, so he finished his beer, flipped his book closed, and padded down the steps. When he got to the bottom of the stairs he nearly fell back in shock.

Standing just inside the front door, dripping wet and sexy as hell, was Melody.

Reece looked at his brother for an explanation, but he only stood there with a stupid grin on his face.

"Hi." Melody's speaking voice was a lovely as her singing voice.

Reece gathered himself and snatched a dirty shirt off the back of the couch. "Hi." He set his empty bottle on the sofa table and slipped the shirt over his head, noticing she hadn't taken her eyes off him as he did it.

"I'm sorry to barge in this late." She swallowed hard and fidgeted with the handle of a rectangular bag she finally held up to show them. "My mom made me this poppyseed chicken casserole, and it's one of four that I'm afraid I'll never be able to eat before it ruins." She tilted her head. "I promise I washed my hands before I touched anything."

Reece ignored Rowen's salivating focus on the casserole and studied her body language. She'd stepped to the side after entering, so to keep with the six-foot social distancing order from the government. Her nerves had given her splotchy hives on her neck and arms, and her clear discomfort suggested she either wasn't used to half-naked men or charity cases. Or lying. Casseroles could be frozen.

"That's very generous of you, Miss…?"

"Landry. I'm Melody Landry. I live across the street." She cleared her throat and tucked her hair behind her ear. "I moved in a few months ago, and I've seen you around, I just haven't made it over to introduce myself yet, so…here I am." She laughed and the expression that followed implied a mental scolding. He couldn't blame her. He wasn't making it easy for her with his awkward silence. He tried to soften his demeanor for her sake and offered a genuine smile.

"Well, Melody, it's nice to meet you. I'm Reece Thomas and this is my brother, Rowen. Welcome to the neighborhood."

"Thanks." Her returning smile brightened the gloomy vibe in their bachelor pad, and Reece knew he could get used to that really fast. He wanted to, in fact. "It's good to be here," she said.

"Are you sure you don't want to freeze your casserole for later?" He looked up through his lashes. "Groceries are scarce these days."

She seemed flustered or nervous, her chest dramatically rising and falling with each breath. She also stayed near the door, subtly backing away from every step Rowen took closer into her six-foot bubble, for which he was thankful, since he could smell the stink wafting off the nasty shirt he'd grabbed. Clearly Rowen had worked out in it earlier today and tossed it on the couch when he was finished. It smelled like chopped onions. Though neither the stench of the sweaty shirt nor the distance prevented her intoxicating smell from reaching him. The rain mixed with her floral scent filled the apartment and nearly brought him to his knees. Reece took a couple of steps back realizing she might be able to smell him after all. Rowen, however, only focused on the food. He held out a hand.

"Here, let me to get that for you."

She stretched her arm out to hand the heavy bag over to him, and they danced a bit trying to maintain an appropriate distance. A jealous twinge pierced through Reece's mood at how close Rowen had gotten to her. He'd definitely broken the social distancing rule. If anyone invaded her bubble, he wanted it to be him.

"Rowen, give her some space. Damn." Rowen gave him a look. Perhaps he'd overreacted a bit, but he didn't care. He nodded toward Melody. "Sorry."

"Oh, it's fine." Melody didn't seem worried

about the invasion as she shook her arm a bit, relieved to be rid of the weight. "My mom said cook it at three-fifty for about half an hour."

"Awesome! Thanks, Mom. Best neighbor ever! Whoo!" Rowen shouted enthusiastically over his shoulder as he disappeared into the kitchen.

Her face split into the most breathtaking happiness Reece had ever seen, and the bubbling laughter plopped a shiny red cherry on top of the beautiful package standing before him.

"Forgive my brother. He is fueled by his stomach." He dipped his chin and grinned, but never removed his gaze from hers. He couldn't even if he'd wanted to. She was mesmerizing. "Thank you for the food."

She shook her head, and he thought a flash of relief briefly crossed her expression. "No, it's fine. Great, in fact. My dad's a doctor, so he's all about health and safety. He and my mom have prepared my kitchen for the Apocalypse, so I have more food in my fridge, freezer, and pantry than I can eat in a year."

"That's very smart of him. The grocery store was like a scene from a dystopian movie, so it's best he saved you from having to fight that mess."

She nodded and looked deeper into his eyes than anyone had in a long time, simultaneously licking her lips, slowly and purposely, nearly causing his sweatpants to tent in appreciation. He didn't blink for fear she would stop, but he was careful not to reveal too much. When she realized she'd been staring too long, she fluttered her lashes and clapped her hands before backing toward the door with a sheepish grin.

"I'll let you two get back to what you were doing before I so rudely interrupted you."

"Hey, you wanna stay and eat with us?" Rowen rounded the corner with two beers and offered her one.

"No, thank you." She backed up a step. "I don't think that would be wise considering the quarantine situation. Besides, I've already eaten, and I have a lot of work to do. I should get back."

"What do you do?" Rowen asked and handed the other beer to Reece.

Reece accepted it, glad his brother was an extrovert and rude enough to pry. He knew what she did but didn't really want her to know he'd Googled her. At least Rowen was a nice buffer to keep him from seeming pathetic and desperate.

"I'm an artist." She beamed. "My collection of paintings was supposed to be auctioned off at an art gallery down the street this week." She glanced nervously at him, piquing his curiosity. "But it's been moved to the internet because of the whole social distancing thing and everyone closing. They're doing a virtual auction on Friday." She rolled her eyes, clearly unimpressed with the new edict. "So, if I want them to sell, I have to go write up everything I would've said about each painting at the show." This woman intrigued him. "I started it, but of course it sucks, so I have to tap into a highly unused portion of my creative mind. Writing."

"I'm sure it will be brilliant." He winked. "We won't keep you." Reece ducked his chin to give her an out. Much to his satisfaction, she hesitated.

"Oh, you're not keeping me. I was actually banging my head against the wall before I came over." A nervous laugh escaped before she composed herself. "Not literally, but metaphorically."

"Why is that?" Reece asked.

"The art director wants me to do a livestream to answer questions people might have about my pieces. I'm not much for live videos. I always come across as a big dork. Like I mentioned before, writing isn't my strength, but I much prefer to be able to think about my answers and have the option to edit and delete stupid comments before they're posted for the world to see, you know?"

Reece nodded slowly. "I do. I'm a musician, so I understand the pressure of performing live."

"Yes." She twisted her hands and avoided eye contact. "I hear you playing sometimes." His cheek lifted with his amusement. "It's beautiful," she murmured. Her adorable embarrassment captured his heart. So genuine.

"Thank you. I, uh, I'm happy to be your test subject if you want to practice. I'm not a writer, but I know my way around a kitchen. I can come over and fix dinner, and you can run through your pitch while you show me your awesome paintings." He held up his palms like a hostage negotiator. "I know we're not supposed to socialize, but I promise, neither of us have been sick or have any symptoms. We've only been to the grocery store once in two weeks and were only there for ten minutes because they were out of everything." He winked. "You're welcome to spray me down with Lysol before I enter your home."

She seemed amused with his reassurance. "I've never been much of a rule-follower anyway. I'd like that." She beamed while intermittently clasping her hands and crossing her arms as if she didn't know what else to do with them. "How do you know my paintings are awesome?"

Damn. Busted. "I saw them when you set them out on the balcony with the banner. Well, two of them, at least. I'd love to see the rest of your collection."

"Oh, yeah." She studied her wet shoes and tucked a lock of hair behind her ear. "I forgot about that," she mumbled through a smirk before looking up and pinning him in place with her big baby blues. "Six tomorrow?" When he didn't answer quickly enough, she amended, "Or you could come earlier. I'm not sure when y'all like to eat. I'm a bit of a night owl."

He rocked back on his heels and winked. "Aren't we all? Six is perfect."

The silence in the room created an intimacy that charged the air, and Rowen's goofy grin harmed now as much as it helped before. She glanced from him to Reece as if suddenly remembering he was there. He offered her casserole bag back to her.

"Thank you. You're a life saver."

"Anytime." She took the bag and looped it over her forearm. "It was great to finally meet y'all." She turned to leave and paused after she opened the door, the rain pelting the pavement just outside the porch. She looked over her shoulder. "If you get hungry, come on over. I have plenty of food, and I'm always home." She shrugged. "I'm not much of a cook, but I wouldn't mind the company."

"Reece is a hell of a cook," Rowen blurted. "I'm sure he would be happy to get his sanitized hands on your"—he smirked—"groceries."

"Ignore him…again." Reece shot an annoyed glance at his brother. "It will be my pleasure to prepare a meal for you. I'll see you tomorrow."

"Great. It's a date then." Her face blanched. "I mean, it's settled. I'll um…" She smiled and bit her bottom lip while scrunching up her adorable nose. "See, live speech isn't my thing." She laughed. "I'll be in touch."

Chapter 7

MELODY STRETCHED BENEATH her chenille blanket when a loud *thud* snapped her to reality. She sat up and looked around, disoriented for a moment. She'd fallen asleep on the sofa. She leaned over to see what had fallen and found her notebook on the wooden floor. She picked it up and reread what she'd written in her stupor after meeting her incredibly handsome neighbors. It wasn't even legible. Gibberish.

Of course it was. How could she possibly concentrate on anything besides the two sexy guys living across her street? Both of them were hot, but Rowen was more the fun, guy-next-door type. Reece, however, had a deep, mysterious, sexy vibe about him that Melody couldn't stop thinking about. Obsessing about. The way he looked at her was almost as if he had X-ray vision and could see right through her. And he wanted to cook for her. A dozen sexy visions flashed in her mind of how that could go. Hand-feeding her olives as he made the salad. Letting her lick the beaters. Melody let out a moan. Ugh. She needed some sex in her life. But not from just anyone. She'd been there and that train-wreck blew up in her face. It had to be Reece. She could feel it in her bones.

When he'd come down the stairs without a shirt, muscles all rippling and flexing as he put on the first shirt his fingers touched… Melody fanned herself. Lord have mercy, he was sexy. She'd caught sight of a huge scar on his abdomen before he slipped the shirt on to cover it. It was too high up to be an appendectomy scar. It could've been from a surgical procedure, but something about the shape made her doubt that. Either way, she'd wanted to assure him he didn't need clothes on her behalf, but she didn't want to come across as desperate. Even though she totally was.

It had been a long time since she'd felt the touch of a man. The last few months of their relationship-wreck were pretty cold. If she was honest with herself, Terry hadn't been much of a giver. He was all take, take, take. What a man Reece Thomas was, with his strong jaw and testosterone practically seeping from his pores. He would most definitely be a giver. He seemed the type to put himself last. She imagined him being insistent she not touch him until after all the plumes of ecstasy had been spent and her needs had been satisfied.

She plopped back on the couch and fantasized about his sexy, dexterous hands all over her in the way he expertly seduced that trumpet. With care and purpose. Smoldering and intense-but-gentle force as he took control and rocked her arousal to her core, making her body tremble with its overdue release. By the time she finished with her erotic daydream, she was as spent as she would've been had he taken over. Maybe. Probably not, but it would be awesome to find out first hand. Who knew hands could be sexy?

She needed answers. Melody grabbed her phone and called her dad. He might know something about him, since he'd been working in the ER for the past five years, and that scar on Reece's abdomen was large enough it would've definitely needed stitches, whether it was a planned surgery or not. Couldn't hurt to ask.

After a lengthy discussion about proper hand washing and sterilization of every surface in her house, she finally managed to ask her dad about Reece. He was surprised he remembered his name and what he had come in for, and even bragged that he had been the doctor to stitch him up, but he didn't know what had happened to Reece that caused the gunshot wound that—thankfully—missed all his vital organs.

So he'd been shot. What other mysteries lay beneath his surface? Maybe she could ask him tonight? Or maybe not. Reece didn't seem like the type to blab about himself much. Rowen, however, seemed more than willing to talk, and he was friendly enough. Though it might be a challenge getting him to divulge private information about his brother. As if the world heard her, Rowen rang the bell. He waved with his hearty smile when he saw her through the glass in the door.

"Hi, neighbor," she greeted.

He held up the casserole dish. "I'm returning your pan, which I personally scrubbed clean."

"Thank you. Wow, you finished it already?"

His eyebrows arched and he guffawed at her shock. "In like…ten minutes."

"No way. The whole thing?"

"The whole thing," he said proudly. "I even shared some with my brother. It was delicious. Thank you."

"Impressive." She nodded with raised brows

and puckered lips. She took the dish from him and stepped aside to let him in. "Please, come in. I was hoping we could chat."

He stepped in and looked around, awe settling into his features. The same expression she had when she'd first seen the place. "Wow. This is amazing. I've always wondered what it looked like in here."

"My grandmother had great taste."

He casually approached her and leaned against the kitchen counter. "So, am I in trouble?"

She felt the line between her brows crease. "No, why would you think that?"

"When a woman tells you she was hoping to chat, that usually means something bad's about to happen."

She rocked her head back and smiled. "Yes, that. I have some questions, and if you don't want to answer it's totally okay." She looked up through her lashes. "About your brother."

He smiled tightly, his lips pressing together like he knew what was coming. "Yeah, I felt that crackling chemistry between you two last night. And now you want to know his story. Why he is so grumpy and anti-social. Am I right?"

"I want to know why he's so sad."

Rowen tilted his head and looked at her

for a few moments before responding. "What makes you think he's sad?"

"He isn't?"

"I didn't say that." He leaned his elbows on her countertop, emphasizing his bulbous muscles and pecs, and looked up at her playfully. "I'm curious how you bet on that emotion out of his roulette wheel of broody behaviors?"

She shrugged one shoulder and searched for the appropriate word to explain her obsession with his brother over the past two months. "I can just tell. The way he moves and speaks." She slowly stepped away from him to look out the window, her hand absently covering her chest, her fingers playing with a button on her blouse. "His music…"

"You like him."

She turned to look at the twisted-yet-suppressed grin. "What's with the Cheshire Cat face?"

"Admit it," he toyed.

Melody hesitated and finally released a sigh-filled, "Yes." She tucked her hair behind her ear and suddenly remembered how awful she must look. She hadn't even seen a mirror yet, or brushed her teeth.

"How? Haven't you just met?" His knowing smile somewhat irritated her, like he already knew the answer but wanted to make her say it aloud. But she was glad someone finally knew. Someone who might be able to help her navigate the stormy seas.

"Well, yes, but…" She dropped her hands to her side and looked anywhere but at him. "It's his music. The songs he chooses, the way he plays them, the emotion that bleeds through the notes pleading for kindness and love. Intimacy. Forgiveness." She faced him, serious as ever. "It speaks to me. It calls to me. The beautiful songs that scream of anguish and heartache. The music that makes me want to cradle his face in my hands and kiss away his pain."

He held up a hand, ending her misery. "I get it. And I think it's cute."

"Cute." She scoffed and swiped away a tear that escaped upon reliving his painful serenades. "His playing is actually what inspired my collection that will be auctioned off this week."

Rowen's eyebrows shot up. "Really? Wow. That's huge." He outstretched his arm, aimed at her with the palm up. "I'm pretty sure he's noticed you as much—if not more—than you have noticed him."

She widened her eyes. This was news to her. Great news. "He's noticed me?"

Rowen's head fell back. "God, you have no idea. He's practically obsessed with you to borderline stalker status." He grinned like the cat that ate the canary. "But he won't admit it to anyone, including himself. You two were made for each other."

They shared a chuckle while she conjured enough courage to ask the most important question. "So, tell me. Why is my apparent soul mate so tragically sad?"

Rowen's joyful expression fell. "This is really his news to tell, but since I know he'll never bring it up, I'll give you the rundown. Three years ago he got a great job at Commander's Palace and started playing in a band on his days off. He married a woman who clearly only saw him as a meal ticket for her gambling addiction, but he refused to listen to our warnings." He flippantly waved his hand in the air, and Melody could tell he still didn't like the girl. "So rather than dumping her like we'd hoped, he eloped and married her. Anyway, one night about two years ago he took my mom and sister out to the Saenger Theater to celebrate, because their birthdays were only two days apart.

"While they were walking in the Quarter, some guy—we think he was a bookie— approached them on a back street and threatened to kill Reece if he didn't pay the debt his wife owed. When my brother told him to piss off in the masterful way only Reece could, the asshole shot my mom. Point blank. That threw my sister—who was a New Orleans police officer—into protector mode, and she lunged for his gun, but he shot her in the chest before she could grab it."

Melody covered her mouth as tears sprang to her eyes. She couldn't imagine experiencing that, or the pain and shock of losing two people you loved dearly in an instant. "Oh my."

"It gets worse. My sister died instantly, but my mom was still alive. Reece had to choose whether to fight the guy or try to help our mom and risk getting shot in the back of his head."

"Which did he choose?" Melody whispered.

Rowen swallowed forcibly, as if choking back emotion. "He's still here, isn't he?"

Melody's stomach twisted as she swallowed back the rising bile. While trying to imagine how one could possibly recover from that, a thought popped into her mind, snapping her out of her reverie. "What about his wife?"

Rowen's frown deepened. "Yeah, that bitch. She divorced him shortly after he got out of the hospital. Claimed he had a hot temper and hit her—which anyone who knows my brother knows that's total bullshit. He's never hit a woman in his life. If nothing else, he's a punching bag for women. Always has been. She was just trying to keep the focus off of her gambling problem that almost got her husband killed. Anyway, she ended up getting her half of everything and ran off with the guitar player from Reece's former band. My brother quit his job and fell into a deep depression."

Rowen picked up a napkin from the counter and started ripping a pattern in it, focusing deeply on the paper as he quietly spoke. "Grief affects different people in different ways. Some move on quickly, others… don't." He shrugged one shoulder. "It's been two years. I mean, it was hard for all of us—my dad and me, too—but, for obvious reasons, Reece took it the hardest." Rowen looked up through his lashes, arching an eyebrow. "He was a Momma's Boy, and…he focused on his napkin again, "Regan was his twin." Melody gasped and covered her gaping mouth with both hands. Rowen crumpled the napkin in his fist. "He blames himself for their deaths."

"That's terrible." Melody was dumbstruck. The unimaginable pain of losing loved ones in such a traumatizing manner, and it was emphasized by the twin connection she'd only ever read about. No wonder his music was so haunting and anguished. He wore his grief like a scarlet letter, shaming himself for not saving them. If she hadn't been falling for him before, she sure was now. "Thank you for telling me all this. It explains so much and helps me understand better."

Rowen tossed the napkin, now in a lovely 3-D snowflake pattern, onto the counter and stood, ruffling her hair like a kid sister. "Don't mention it. I hope you and Reece hit it off. He needs a sweet girl like you. He deserves to be happy again. But, word to the wise, I wouldn't let him know I told you all this stuff. He's weird about people knowing his shit." He paused at the door before he left and gave his signature crooked grin. "I think my mom and sister would have liked you." He stole a squirt of the hand sanitizer she had placed by the entry and winked before closing the door behind him.

That was all she needed to hear to finalize her decision. When Reece came over later she would make sure their evening was full of romance, talk of art and music, and seducing each other with their words and touch-less actions. Then, when the mood was perfect, she would make him an offer he couldn't refuse. One that would involve plenty of touching. Melody ducked into the bathroom and brushed her teeth and hair so she wouldn't scare people if anyone else ignored the quarantine law and happened to stop by.

After lunch, Melody tried to get in the zone and work on her presentation, but the thoughts just weren't flowing. She wished Reece would bust out his trumpet and get her creative juices flowing. She walked out onto her balcony and looked around, blown away by what lay before her.

Because of the pandemic, the streets were not only empty like the time she'd looked before, but now they were bare and washed clean for the first time in Melody's twenty-four years. Daniel was right. Her beautiful city was like a ghost town. Most of the time. There were still a few brave—or foolish—souls walking the Quarter, but all were spread a great distance from each other.

Was this virus everything the media was claiming? She didn't personally know of anyone who had it, nor did she know anyone who personally knew someone infected with it. Surely it wasn't as bad as people were claiming. She hoped neither she nor Reece or Rowen were asymptomatic, though their proximity the past few days had risked infecting each other. After all, if any of them had the virus, they'd probably already shared it anyway by entering each other's houses. But they seemed healthy enough and said they hadn't been out much. She hadn't left the condo in weeks, so… Being with him was worth the risk, she decided.

She allowed herself a few more moments of solace before finishing the presentation she would perform for Reece tonight. In her condo. Alone. And possibly naked.

Chapter 8

REECE FUSSED OVER his outfit like he was a teenager about to go on a first date with his first crush. Never mind he was a divorcé hoping to score with a girl he'd fallen for after only actually speaking to her once. Score. Reece shook his head and scoffed at himself. Which idiot was he, Beavis or Butthead? He'd already changed clothes three times. To literally go across the street. Honestly, with the connection he felt with Melody, she probably wouldn't even notice what he wore.

He'd already checked with Melody to make sure she had all the ingredients he needed to make Chicken Piccata for dinner, accompanied by roasted veggies, a hearty salad, and fresh-baked rolls, and told her what all he would need. And, of course, a chilled Sauvignon Blanc to accompany the perfect meal.

Reece sipped from his high-ball glass, allowing the top-shelf whisky to burn some liquid courage into his bloodstream. At least he had a nice stash of his favorite brand built up before COVID-19 decided to warp the earth. Tonight would be special. He'd see to it. For the first time in two years, he approved the face looking back at him in the mirror. There might even be a little spark in those eyes again.

He gathered the bundle of blooms he'd cut from a flowering tree in the courtyard of his apartment building, and he practically skipped out the door, waving to Rowen on his way out.

"Stay out of your own damn head!" Rowen shouted through a mouthful of pork and beans as Reece shut the door. What did that mean? He knew but ignored it anyway. His brother had a point. The only person standing in the way of his happiness was him. Perhaps Melody was the key to unlock the vault he had shoved his joy into when heartache burrowed its way into his life.

Melody's warm greeting and incredible, feminine scent hit him before her voice did. She stepped aside so he could enter the expansive foyer, and wow. Just wow. He'd seen portions of the inside through the windows, but it didn't compare to actually standing in it. The winding staircase that hugged the wall looked like something straight out of a palace. Fitting for its Royal Street address.

"The wine is chilled, and the kitchen is this way." Melody waved her hand like a flight attendant pointing out the exit doors. "Are those for me?" She nodded toward the flowers.

"Oh, yes." He handed them to her. She leaned forward and kissed his cheek, causing a kaleidoscope of butterflies to attack his chest cavity. It would've been so easy to turn his cheek at the last minute to kiss her luscious mouth, but he resisted. Clearly sharing germs wasn't an issue for her, but no need to ruin things before they ever get started.

"Thank you. They're beautiful." She took the flowers into the kitchen, and he followed. He looked over the groceries scattered across the counter-top while she clipped the stems of the flowers and put them in a vase of water. "I set out the ingredients you texted me earlier. My island looks like I'm about to film a cooking show." She giggled, igniting his soul. If he never heard another sound in his life, he'd be okay. "Gotta say, it's probably a first for this place. My grandmother never cooked as long as I knew her."

That blew his mind. "How did she eat?"

Melody sat for a moment pondering and

puckered her lips in thought. "I think she either had take-out, went to a friend's house, or had people cook for her. She was quite the socialite."

"Sounds like it." He tied an apron around his waist. "How about you. Do you take after your grandmother?"

"Me? No. I'm a stereotypical introverted artist all the way. I inherited her cooking skills, though. My mom tried to teach me when I was younger, but I burned everything. How did you learn to cook?"

"I went to culinary school right out of high school. I always enjoyed helping my mom prepare meals, and it turns out I had a knack for it."

"Wow. Rowen said you worked at Commander's Palace, but I didn't realize you were an actual chef. I figured you were a waiter or host. How did you manage to get a job at the ritziest restaurant in New Orleans? That's pretty incredible."

What the hell? When had she discussed his career with Rowen? And why was his brother blabbing about Reece's life to her? He sucked in a calming breath.

"Yeah." He finished preparing the chicken to cook and popped an olive from the salad into his mouth. "Luck, I guess. Right place, right time kind of thing." He turned to gather the rest of the salad ingredients so his back was to her and she wouldn't see the annoyance on his face. "When did you see Rowen?"

She hesitated. Why did she hesitate? "Oh, he brought my dish back this morning." She reached around him to grab the salad dressing from the cupboard, and her breasts brushed against his back, making him completely forgive Rowen's big mouth. "I may have asked about you while he was here." She gave a sly grin, her face inches from his, and he watched her pupils dilate beneath heavy lids. He had to stop being paranoid. Before he could make a move, she'd slipped away to get some wineglasses from a different cabinet.

"So what else did my big-mouth brother tell you?"

Her back was still toward him, and she simply shrugged. "Not too much. That you used to work at Commander's Palace and play in a band." She turned, her face alight with intrigue, blue eyes sparkling. "Did you ever meet Emeril Lagassé? I've heard he pops in a lot."

Reece couldn't help but put his grievance with Rowen aside and chuckle at the wonder on her face. "I did. He actually cooked alongside me a few times." Reece put the dredged chicken into the hot skillet and adjusted the heat beneath it. While it sizzled its savory soundtrack, he prowled toward her like a panther on the hunt. "He also taught me a few things about wine."

He'd backed her against the counter, their hips touching, and reached behind her to get the Sauvignon Blanc she'd retrieved from the cooler. She'd stopped breathing when he'd bent over her to reach it, and their bodies were practically pressed together while he poured two glasses. The sexual tension between them was palpable. He pulled back a little, but not before handing her the glass and sipping from his own. He practically felt her heart pounding in her chest from their heated proximity. A vein pulsed in her neck, begging him to press his lips to it, and perhaps run his tongue down the column of her sexy throat.

As quickly as he'd encroached her space, he left it to tend to his skillet full of chicken. He would swear he caught her fanning herself.

While they ate, Reece caught her staring at him a few times when she thought he wasn't looking. That sent a thrill zipping through his body like a 480 volt charge. He had to force himself to stop bouncing his leg beneath the table.

"So, where did you learn to sing so well?"

Her eyes widened. "What?"

He mocked innocence. "What, you're the only one allowed to eavesdrop on someone's musical gifts?"

Her face flooded with her embarrassment, and she pressed two fingers to her forehead, trying to hide her face. He pulled her hand away and squeezed gently.

"Hey, your voice is incredible. It inspires me. Why do you think my windows are always open during allergy season when the trees are spooging their seed everywhere?"

That made her laugh and seemed to relax her enough to answer. "My mom sings in the choir at church, and she's taught me everything she knows."

"Lucky me. I look forward to your serenades."

"Not as much as I do yours."

Chapter 9

BY THE TIME they finished their amazing meal, Melody was way too full to eat dessert. How she'd had an appetite for anything other than sex was beyond her, but the way he offered little tidbits of knowledge while he prepared everything, and giving her tastes after telling her what flavors to look for and concentrate on—that in itself was erotic. Either that, or the wine was getting to her. She didn't much care. All she wanted to do was feel his touch and learn whatever else he was willing to teach her.

"Do you want to see my paintings?"

"Sure. You can practice on me."

She'd like to practice plenty on him, but for now her sales pitch was good enough. They walked to the formal living room where she'd had her paintings set up for the photographer beneath the track lighting, and she switched on the lights. He threaded his fingers through hers while they walked the length of the display as if at an art show, and she explained the premise behind each painting, watching his responses carefully.

He was probably the only person in the world who'd ever truly listened to her intently and passionately. Looking so deeply into her eyes like he wanted to know everything that went into the thought behind each brush stroke. She probably got a little carried away describing the inspiration and story behind each scene, but he didn't seem to mind. Then they got to the last painting. He stared at the trumpet player, recognition filling his features.

"And this one?"

"The Royal Lullaby." She suddenly felt embarrassed by what she had painted. For using him so intimately without his permission. "I had gone through a dry spell for several years. Kind of like writer's block, but for painting. I couldn't think of anything I wanted to paint. Then, one day, I was fresh out of a breakup, sulking on my chaise lounge about wasting three good years of my life with an asshole who clipped my wings and caused me to lose my spark and passion for painting."

She looked at him and felt a smile bloom

across her face. "And that's when I heard the most beautiful sound coming from outside. Not just any sound. Haunting anguish and pain, a sadness that can only be felt and not heard. It was incredible and represented exactly what I was feeling at the time. Exactly what I needed to paint." He looked at her with a peculiar expression, head tilted, and speculative eyes. "So I scurried to my studio and painted the first scene in my collection. My version of the hurt that trumpet portrayed." She pulled his hand to her mouth and kissed the back of it. "You are my muse."

"I shall wear the title like a badge of honor."

Melody reached up and caressed his face, running her finger along the deep-seated frown lines. "Who knew the amount of beauty that could come from an outpouring of grief?"

His eyes crinkled in the corners a bit. "What makes you so sure it was grief?"

She tilted her chin. "The music. It speaks for itself." Melody grabbed her wineglass from the nearby table. "Ready for a refill?"

Reece's cheek lifted with a half grin that didn't reach his eyes. He nodded and gathered the dirty dishes from the table. She followed him to the kitchen with their empty wineglasses.

"Looks like we killed the bottle of Blanc." Melody dropped the empty bottle in the recycle bin while he rinsed the dishes in the sink to load them into the dishwasher.

"We could open another if you'd like?" he said over his shoulder.

Enough with the verbal foreplay and sexual tension. It was her turn to seduce him. "I can think of better things to do." She slinked her arms around his waist from behind him while he ran the plates under the faucet. He stiffened when her hand neared the place where his scar was on his abdomen. She'd forgotten it was there until his reaction, and she quickly moved her palms lower. He dropped his head back and sucked in a breath. The next thing she knew, her fingers were threading through his and he was spinning her around in a dance where she landed perfectly in his embrace.

He leaned close to her face, their noses nearly touching, and paused. "Me, too."

Her gaze shifted from his mouth to his eyes, but his never left her mouth. Tired of waiting for him to make his move, she leaned upward and rejoiced in the explosion of sensuality from their moist lips that fit together like puzzle pieces. Searing hot, wet, wanton puzzle pieces that moved together in perfect sync and rhythm, igniting every pheromone present in the air around them.

Somehow, they'd made it to her sofa, glided over the back of it like an Olympic high jumper without ever breaking their connection, and landed shirtless atop one another. His hands—his perfect, dexterous, sexy hands—deftly unclasped her bra with shocking ease and traced the underside of her breast with a forefinger, leaving a trail of heat along her skin. She watched his washboard abs ripple from the exertion of keeping the brunt of his weight off her and debated licking every contour between the ridges. But then her eyes landed on the six-inch scar just above his waistline.

His hands stilled when he noticed where her attention focused. He sat back a bit and looked at her as if expecting her to say something. She didn't know what to say, so she blurted the first thing that came to mind.

"Does it hurt?" She traced a fingertip across the shiny, white scar tissue causing him to flinch.

"No, but it's still sensitive to the touch."

"Sorry." She moved her fingers to trace the outline of his abs, but somehow the mood had shifted.

"It's fine." He eyed her speculatively. "You know, most people would follow with 'What happened?'" His lips tightened. "But something tells me you already know. What else did my brother tell you?"

Crap. This must be what Rowen had warned her about. She needed to throw him off the scent. "Nothing. Just that you were wounded and still recovering."

Reece dropped his head and pinched the bridge of his nose, shaking his head. "Right. I'll bet that's all his big ass mouth said. You don't have to protect him." He sat up, sliding off of her, and rested his elbows on his knees. "I'll bet he just couldn't wait to dish about my tragic life."

Melody rushed to put her shirt back on over her bra-less boobs. He was clearly angry. *Way to ruin the moment, Mel.* "Honestly, it was my fault. Please don't be upset with him. I had asked him to tell me about you after I saw the scar, but he didn't tell me anything I couldn't have found out on my own." She sat up and smiled proudly. "My dad is actually the surgeon who operated on you when you went to the emergency room."

He gave her a side eye, but the twitching jaw muscles gave away his anger. "So what, you got the scoop from your dad and couldn't wait to save the neighborhood charity case? So much for privacy laws. Guess those don't count when it's your daughter asking." He grabbed his shirt and slipped it on in one fluid motion while standing. "I don't want your pity." He stalked toward her front door while she chased after him.

"Wait, please! This isn't pity. I've already told you how I feel about you." He stopped and turned to her, nearly causing her to collide into him. "I told you I fell in love with you before I ever saw your face. Much less your story."

"Love at first sight is a farce. There is only lust and infatuation. Something I usually deprive myself of for fear of *this* happening."

How dare he discount her feelings so flippantly without recognizing and owning his own issues.

"Bullshit," she spat. "If we're tossing out judgment here, let's be honest all the way around. You're afraid of opening yourself up to let anyone in for fear of losing them like you lost your mom and sister."

"Shut up, Melody." Reece's face crumpled. "Damn Rowen for always butting into my life."

"No. You're lucky to have someone who gives a shit about you. He loves you and wants you to find happiness, which—let's be honest—is what you've been depriving yourself of, not lust and infatuation. You are scared because you finally found someone you care about who makes you happy and actually gets you, and you don't know how to handle it. So, you're pushing me away and blaming it on Rowen."

Reece jerked open the door. "You don't know anything about me."

She shook her head through the blinding tears. "You're wrong."

"Good bye, Melody."

He slammed the door behind him and darted off around the corner in the opposite direction of his front door. She worried for his safety considering the stressful pandemic situation and desperation of people looking for an individual alone in the dark. She closed her eyes and tried to blot out the wounded expression that flashed across his face just before he left. She really did love him, dammit. Despite what her head was screaming, her heart couldn't let him go.

Chapter 10

THREE DAYS. THREE days had passed and she still hadn't heard from Reece. She'd become obsessed, watching for his movement in his apartment, worrying if she'd ruined everything, but she never saw him coming or going. He could've been there, he could've not. She had no idea. Thursday came and went, and he didn't perform on his balcony. The first Thursday he'd missed in two months.

She'd dropped a few more casseroles off with Rowen, but he wouldn't tell her anything. He simply thanked her and closed the door. Reece must've chewed him out pretty badly for spilling the beans. Why'd she have to slip and reveal that she knew anything? She was the one with the big mouth.

Melody's phone buzzed, and through her bleary, tear-streaked vision she could make out Daniel's name flashing across the screen. *Dammit*. She wasn't ready. She'd sent her written descriptions for the website yesterday but still had to finalize what she would say live as an introduction and a conclusion, selling herself and why people would be better off with one of her paintings in their homes.

"Hey, Daniel."

"Hey, stunner. How does it feel to be on top?"

Her confusion infiltrated the silence. "Huh? What does that even mean?"

"You're donating the proceeds of your sales to the hospital to buy more medical equipment for this pandemic, right?"

"Yeah. Why?" Melody's stomach sank. "What's going on?"

"So the auction is no longer an auction. It's just an art show now."

"What?" she shrieked. Had they pulled her from the auction thinking she wouldn't draw enough money? "Why? My work is plenty good enough to draw people in and get some bids. Don't do this."

"Whoa, whoa, it's not that."

"Then what is it? Because it sounds like you're pulling me from the whole auction."

"Mel, haven't you looked at the website this morning?"

The Royal Muse

"No, I didn't even know it was up yet. I haven't submitted my descriptions or anything." She snatched her notebook from the table and sorted through her scratch notes. "I can email them to you now if you want—"

"No need. So, you know I uploaded the pics the photographer took day before yesterday—they were spectacular, by the way—because the auction went live at six this morning."

"Six? Daniel! Why didn't you tell me?"

"Well, we were going to, but since this was our first time doing anything like this we kind of went by the seat of our pants. I wanted to make sure it would upload correctly and all that before people would come looking. Anyway, all that doesn't matter. Less than an hour after it went live, someone bought all your paintings."

The breath whooshed out of Melody's lungs. "What?" she managed to squeak out. "I thought it was an auction. Bidding and all that?"

"It was going to be, but he offered more than the bid amount, so we waited a couple of hours to see if anyone showed any interest in outbidding. Honestly, with the fear going around and panic-buying, we were worried people might be hesitant to shell out the dough, you know? So we closed the auction and are now just showcasing your collection for publicity."

"But… How…" She honestly didn't know what to say.

"It's the fastest sales we've ever had in the history of this art gallery. We may have to do this virtual thing more often. Congratulations, Mel! That's quite an accomplishment."

"W-who bought them?"

"I don't have the information yet. I only have an email address. Whoever it is, they're definitely your biggest fan."

Warmth spread through her. She had a suspicion but needed to be sure. "What's the email address?"

"Uh, hang on. I printed out the transaction." Daniel sorted through papers. "Here it is. Lonely trumpeter at gmail dot com. Oh wait, there is a name." Melody knew who it was before Daniel ever read it. "Someone named Reece Thomas."

Mother Nature herself couldn't stop the flash flood of tears. Three days after she thought he'd walked out of her life forever, Reece had bought her collection before anyone else had an opportunity. And for who knows how much money? Maybe he didn't hate her as much as she'd thought.

Movement from her front door caught her

attention, and she looked up from her notebook and into the eyes of the soul that had captivated her without a word. Reece nodded and waved as if he was afraid to disturb her.

"Daniel, I gotta go." She dropped her phone without even checking to see if she'd hung up, and then sprinted to the front door. She took a deep breath before opening it.

"Hey." She cringed at how breathless her voice sounded.

"Hey."

Unspoken words flowed between them as they just gazed into each other's eyes. He finally broke the silent communication.

"You were right," he said. "I'm scared."

She nodded but didn't speak.

"I'm sorry for the things I said."

She nodded again.

"I don't want a fling. I want all of you all the time. I want to feed you, support you, sit with you. I want to lay in the grass and feed you strawberries, play music for you while you paint, hold you when you're sad and let your tears wash away my own grief. I want to be with you, take afternoon naps, and do stupid shit that nobody else gets but us. I want to make love to you. Melody, I…"

She lunged forward and pressed her lips to his. He wrapped her up and kissed her stupid. By the time they came up for air, both of them were panting and had no reason for further conversation. They could talk later. For now, they had a symphony to perform.

The End

Connect with Judy

SOCIAL LINKS

https://www.Judy-McDonough.com

https://www.goodreads.com/judymcdonough

http://www.pinterest.com/Judy_McDonough

http://www.facebook.com/JudyMcDonoughAuthor

http://www.facebook.com/groups/TheBayouKrewe

http://twitter.com/JudyMcDonough

http://www.instagram.com/Judy_Mack

Read More By Judy

The Bayou Secrets Saga:
Deadline (Book 1)
Lifeline (Book 2)
Flatline (Book 3)
Kristy's Runway

About the Author

Judy is an award-winning author of the paranormal romance series titled: The Bayou Secrets Saga. Her latest novel, Kristy's Runway, is a contemporary romance about her secondary characters from the Saga. Due for release in summer 2020.

Judy is a U. S. Navy veteran and has moved more as a civilian than she ever did as an active duty sailor. A native Arkansan, she's now settled in northern Georgia where she plans to stay put for at least a decade 'cause she's tired of moving. She's lived all over the South (and a brief stint in NE Ohio), but nowhere captured her like New Orleans. Most of her stories are cradled in the Crescent City or deep in the heart of the bayou.

When she isn't writing, she's probably listening to jazz music, relaxing outside in her hammock, cooking, or sipping a cocktail on the patio with her husband. Judy has three ridiculously handsome and kind sons—and a good, sturdy broomstick ready to use if needed—that offer plenty of shenanigans material for her books.

Follow Judy at *www.Judy-McDonough.com* for more information, the latest updates, and new releases.

Join her Facebook group, *The Bayou Krewe,* for more personal interaction.

Check out her Bayou Secrets Saga for another juicy taste of the bayou.